❀THE STORY OF A COLONIAL GIRL❀

Emma's Journal

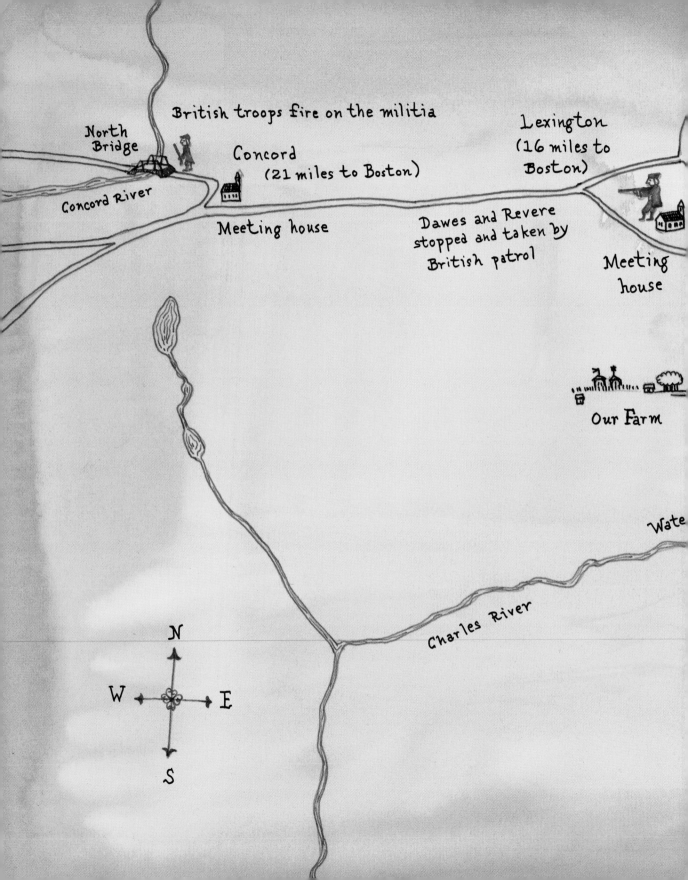

1 2

3 4

5 6

The Manual Exercise of the Foot Guards

Amos gave
me this page from
the militia's training
manual.

❈THE STORY OF A COLONIAL GIRL❈

Emma's Journal

by
Marissa Moss

SCHOLASTIC INC.
New York Toronto London Auckland Sydney
Mexico City New Delhi Hong Kong

To Lori and Sara

The Boston Tea Party

July 18, 1774

The house is hush and still. I should be asleep, like everyone else, but I am too excited, so I have taken my journal to the windowsill and write by the light of the full moon. Tomorrow I leave our farm in Menetomy and go to Boston, such a big, bustling city. I have never been there, but Daddy says 'tis a fine, fancy city, with cobbled streets, stores heaped with rich goods, and not one church but nine! I would go with all my heart if Daddy, Mamma, or even my little sister, Mercy, should stay with me, but I will be alone. Except, of course, for Aunt Harmony ~ 'tis for her sake I go. She has no serving girl since the British blockaded Boston. (This past winter Americans dumped British tea into the harbor to protest the new tea tax. Daddy called it a "tea party," but with the blockade as punishment, no one feels festive now.) All of Aunt's boarders but one, Thankful Bliss, have left as well, fearful of the British troops that have taken over the city. I should think I should be fearful, too, but Daddy says we are good subjects of the King and have no cause to fret, especially not 10~year~old girls. I pray he is right. I look at Mercy, her face silver like an angel in the moonlight, and I wish I could stay with her always.

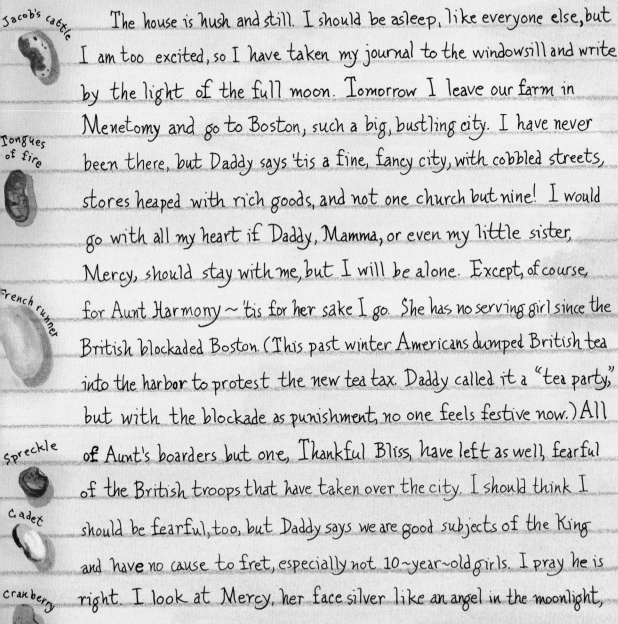

bring many provisions from our farm to Aunt~ lots of beans.

Mercy asleep in our bed

The city is as lively and fashionable as Daddy said. People dressed in London styles stroll the clean streets, and vendors hawk pies, eggs, and butter despite the blockade.

July 23, 1774

I woke in a strange room in a strange house to the sounds of fife and drum as the regulars drilled on the common. How I long for birdsong and the peaceful chirping of crickets! I miss the fresh country air and my dear Mamma and Daddy, Mercy, and my brothers, John, Paul, and Duncan. I feel out of place in this big, strange city, and out of sorts in this house.

Aunt Harmony is a dear soul but a harsh taskmaster. Already I am spinning, carding, weaving, and sewing (enow, I should think, to clothe an entire regiment!). Woe to me should I allow my shoulders to rest upon a chair's back ~ such luxury is for gentlemen and the elderly alone. Thankful slumps until she hears Aunt's footfalls, then she jerks upright, immediately proper.

Aunt Harmony loves to speak in proverbs, and they all have to do with thrift and hard work.

> Idle hands are the devil's playground.

> Waste not, want not.

> Many hands make light work.

This distance spans higher than from forehead to chin!

Thankful puts me in mind of a doll with a fine bisque head. I hope her head proves to be less hollow, but all I can tell so far is that she cares much for fashion. She wears a stylish hair roll, though she complains it makes her head itch and burn.

Thankful is 14 years old, and her uncle sent her to Boston to be educated. Her parents are both dead and her bachelor uncle cannot teach her the necessary refinements.

'Tis not as desperate here as I feared, so much food and money comes in by the charity of other towns, even other colonies.

Virginia has sent bushels of corn, wheat, and flour.

South Carolina sent rice and money.

Even Quebec shipped thousands of bushels of wheat.

July 28, 1774

Dr. Joseph Warren came to tea today. Aunt is very proud of her tea

service as 'twas made by Paul Revere, a fine silversmith, and, like Dr. Warren,

a noted Son of Liberty. I call it tea, but we drink coffee or chocolate ~

Aunt is a staunch Whig and boycotts all British goods.

Dr. Warren is a fine, handsome gentleman, elegantly dressed

and wearing a brown tie wig (which I much prefer to powdered hair ~

how it makes me sneeze!). Aunt dotes on him, but Thankful distrusts

him as she is a fierce Tory while he thinks the colonies should govern

themselves without England's interference. Thankful says the patriots are

"low rabble" who want mob rule, but Dr. Warren is no ruffian. He is

charming and interesting. Talking with him I feel I understand the world

better. (And elsewise it seems such a muddle. Are we British or American?

What does it mean to be a Whig or a Tory? Dr. Warren says we can support

the King but must first stand up for ourselves.)

Dr. Warren told a story about a country man entering Boston who was near 8 feet tall. His size astonished the sentries on duty who were already surprised by the many colonists near 6 feet tall. The country man laughed at the regulars. "Ay," he said, "ye do not know what boys there be in this country ~ I am one of the smallest!"

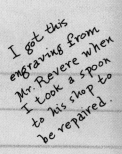

August 3, 1774

A letter at long last from Mamma and Daddy! Little Mercy is spinning on the big wheel. Brothers John, Duncan, and Paul have got in the rye and most of the hay. They have joined the militia and must drill every week. There was a fine cornhusking frolic. Duncan found a red ear and claimed a kiss from Nabby ~ I knew he was sweet on her!

Glad as I was to have news from home, it made me feel dumpish to read it, so much do I miss my dear ones and the farm. I try to think of Thankful as a sister, but I know she thinks me a clumsy country dolt. While I spin and weave, she studies piano and penmanship. Why should my hands be red and raw from scrubbing while hers are soft, white lady hands?

August 23, 1774

Work, work, work, from dawn to dusk, a catalog of tasks. Always the same: spin, weave, card, milk cows, tend cows, build up fires, cook, clean, make cheese, churn butter, embroider, wash, iron, strew fresh sand on the kitchen floor ~ all with the sameness of a clock ticking, not even a song to cheer me up unless I sing it myself. 'Tis nought but drudgery!

I miss going to the schoolhouse, playing with the other pupils, running about the farm with Mercy at my heels. Here my world is reduced to this house and the whims of Aunt Harmony. 'Tis an endless list of chores. I hear her voice in my sleep even. Sometimes I think I shall scream, working like an ox while Thankful idly thumbs through a lady's magazine.

> Polish this. Sweep that. 'Tis a stain I see? Wash it out well. Peel the potatoes. Chop some kindling. Do we need more soap made?

August 28, 1774

Aunt Harmony went out visiting today (quilting at Sarah Owens's), so Thankful proposed we go walking together. I was delighted to do so, free from Aunt's watchful eye and flattered that the stylish Thankful would consider me suitable company. If only she would be a friend and not act such a schoolmarm, always lecturing me. We walked to John Hancock's fine mansion, and Thankful pointed out the homes she knew, where various balls and diversions had been held. Then we came to a house that had been daubed in "Hillsborough Paint" ~ that is, the reeking contents of privies and chamberpots had been smeared on the walls.

"This is how your Sons of Liberty treat merchants who import British goods," Thankful said sharply, as if I had done the deed.

"Aunt and Dr. Warren both say 'tis wrong to profit off our misery by selling British wares," I retorted.

Thankful narrowed her eyes and lips ~ she looked a very snake ~ and

gold guinea

copper halfpenny

hissed, "'Tis they who cause misery, not the poor merchant!"

I do not know truly who was in the right, but the day, which had started out so fine, was ruined. We walked home without speaking a word. And I shall not be the first to speak ~ I promise!

September 15, 1774

I have found a friend in Amos, our neighbor. He fishes in the harbor (but the regulars allow it only so long as he sells most of his catch to them). He is so cheery and full of news, I relish his visits. I suspect he is sweet on Thankful, but he is also sweet to me.

It has been near 3 months since I left home and I miss my family terribly, so I asked Amos if he could take me for a short visit. (Aunt said 'twas fine with her.) But when we came to the city gates, the sentries refused to let us pass without a permit. Off we went to military headquarters to procure the needed document, but all I procured was a stiff back and sore bum from sitting on a hard bench, waiting, waiting, waiting. Finally Major Small deigned to see me and I begged leave to see my family. He did not even glance my way but said, "No."

After waiting so long, I could not leave it at that. "But why, sir?" I protested. "I am a mere child. What danger can I be to His Majesty's army?"

Amos

"I said no," he repeated, and this time he did look at me, <u>glaring</u>. "Because you are saucy and do not know your place. Is it the air you breathe that makes you colonists so impertinent? Even a young maid dares to sass an officer? Out with you ~ you have wasted enough of my time!"

I dared not murmur a word. I ran out, crying. Would I <u>never</u> see Mamma and Daddy again? Was Boston a city or a prison?

Amos said 'twas our timing that was bad ~ the regulars just seized some fieldpieces from the militia in Cambridge and in response guns were stolen from the British battery in Boston (right under the sentries' noses!). The officers now suspect everyone of preparing for an armed rebellion. Will arms really be taken up?

September 20, 1774

The sound of the spinning wheel as it goes round is a sad, low, monotonous hum. I sit and spin and spin and sit, imagining the thread is a line stretching all the way home, binding me to Mamma at her own spinning wheel.

October 3, 1774

me

Dr. Warren came to tea (I mean coffee) and brought with him our friend Amos who has taken it into his head to woo Thankful. To please her (or so he thought),

Mamma

he dressed up like a dandy, powdered hair and all! She was polite as could be while he stayed, but as soon as he left, she dissolved into giggles, so foolish did he look. We sang the Macaroni song all evening:

"This fashion who does e'er pursue, I think a simpleton-y;
For he's a fool, say what you will, who is a Macaroni."

October 12, 1774

Thankful blows hot and cold, now sweet to me, now bitter. Oftimes she treats me like a servant or a child too young for her to notice. Other days she plaits my hair and shares the pastilles her uncle sends her. Today 'twas bitter, and when she set out on a walk, she said she did not want my company. Well, I did not care a dried apple! Was I suddenly too dull, too country oafish for her? She would not answer, but swept out in her good silk shawl. So I followed her in secret. She met with a foppish officer, and I thought, "She is a British spy!" But from the blushes and fluttering lashes, 'twas clear they were sparking, and the only secrets traded were those of the heart.

I stayed and watched awhile and was about to go when a runaway horse came clattering down the cobblestones. The horse knocked Thankful down. Her officer rushed to help her up. She was unharmed, but her proudest attribute, her hair roll, suffered mortally! The outer covering of hair was thrust aside

and the stuffing of tow, cotton, and false hair fell out.

A crowd of jeering boys fell upon the stuffing, kicking it and pelting
one another with it. Thankful was in tears, but oh, how I laughed!

Hairstyles of the Illustrious and Wealthy

white for formal dress

rolled hair

tied bob

brown for every day

ringlets

gray for business

Thankful is so proud of
her hair roll, she sleeps
sitting up with a specially
built box over her hair
so as not to disturb the
perfect shape. So much
discomfort in the name
of Beauty!

October 14, 1774

So it now seems the hair roll is no longer stylish. Or so Thankful
claimed when I asked her why she no longer wears it. Will her beau
still like her now she is wearing ringlets? At least her neck will
not be stiff from sleeping upright, which should improve her disposition.

November 2, 1774

Thankful asked Aunt if she could have a guest to tea today (though
our "teas" are quite simple of late ~ no cream cakes or sweet biscuits).
When Aunt heard the guest was a British soldier, she got herself
into a pucker and insisted she would die before being hostess to a
lobsterback.

Thankful stamped her foot and glared that poisonous look of hers.

I finished my sampler during Thankful's tantrum.

I chose the motto from a saying of Benjamin Franklin's. If I cannot be a Son of Liberty, then I shall be a Daughter!

Thankful could help churn butter or make cheese. At least 'tis clean work and sweet smelling. (I love marking the butter with different prints.)

butter

cheese

(What a willful, spoiled creature!) "You are a petty tyrant and a traitor to the King!" she hissed.

Aunt Harmony is rarely speechless, but she was then, appalled to hear such disrespectful language (and from such a "refined lady"). Her mouth opened and closed like a fish, jowls atwitch with outrage.

Thankful blushed a deep scarlet, mortified by her own words. "Please forgive me, madam," she beseeched, kneeling with bowed head. "My temper got the better of me, but it shall not happen again."

I hoped Aunt would settle her hash and lock her in her room. (Even better if she made her work in the kitchen ~ that would take Miss~ High~and~Mighty down a peg or two.) But Aunt seemed exhausted by the ordeal and waved Thankful away. Was that to be all? I wanted some way to punish Thankful.

"Perhaps Thankful had best miss tea altogether," I suggested.

Aunt frowned. "These are confusing times and neighbor is set against neighbor, husband set against wife. I do not agree with Thankful's loyalist views ~ nor with her rudeness ~ but I refuse to let our differences

I miss our good fall apples and the cider Mamma makes. What I would give for her apple pie!

Carolina Sweet   Rennet   Normandy   Maidenblush   Ribston   Rambo   Russet   Cooper Russet

poison this household. We shall treat each other civilly." Aunt arched a thin

eyebrow in that annoying way she has. "Which means you shall treat Thankful

like the lady she is."

"Of course, Aunt Harmony," I murmured, but if I were to treat

Thankful as she merits, I would paddle her backside.

November 18, 1774

The usual Thanksgiving feast was sparse this year, and the company was not

loud nor merry. Amos, no longer a Macaroni (does he, too, know of Thankful's

trysts with the officer?), joined us for dinner and dear Dr. Warren stopped

by for pie and coffee. But there was no Mamma, Daddy, Mercy, or brothers

to lift a glass with, and I felt low, not "thankful" at all.

December 3, 1774

It has been weeks since I set pen to paper, but there is nothing to

note. As 'tis this journal is not much use. I thought 'twould be a short

record of a fascinating sojourn in lively Boston, and here 'tis ~ a

boring string of weeks in a captivity of sorts. The prison is spacious

but a prison nonetheless. I hear intriguing snippets from Amos and

Dr. Warren ~ plans to move cannon or gather ammunition. But when

I pester Amos to know more, he says 'tis safer for me to know nothing,

which just piques my curiosity the better. I am shut outside (or, rather,

'Tis bad enough that Thankful treats me like a babe in swaddling clothes, but Amos, too?

Thankful was radiant on the arm of her beau. Why does she get everything she desires?

inside the house) while others act. Can I do nothing worthwhile?

January 18, 1775

Today the troops celebrated the Queen's birthday. There was a parade, military displays, much rumpumpum band music, and General Gage hosted a grand gala, to which Thankful went on the arm of her spark. His name, I now know, is George Prentiss and he is with the Royal Marines. Thankful has taken me into her confidence (who else has she?), and as we sit and embroider, she describes the many talents and charms of George.

I was naturally <u>not</u> invited to the ball, but I could not bear staying at home when finally something Exciting was happening. So I stole out of bed and followed the throng to the General's house. I thought, "This must be what London is like," so many coaches drove up carrying finely dressed gentlemen and ladies. All the windows of the house were lit bright as day, and I crept up to one for a peek. There were so many British officers, I thought I might overhear important news (for once, I would have something to tell Amos!), but all I learned was Mrs. Quincy's recipe for punch. Still, 'twas like a fairy story, all glittering chandeliers, gilt mirrors, stately men, and bejeweled ladies. I confess, the splendor made me wish myself a Tory like Thankful. Why must I be ever on the edge of things, never a part of anything?

dancing shoes

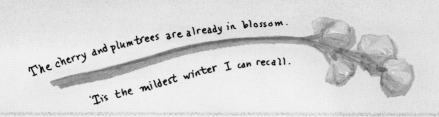

The cherry and plum trees are already in blossom.

'Tis the mildest winter I can recall.

February 18, 1775

A letter from Mamma and Daddy! Or should I say news from them, since 'twas not truly a letter but writing on the margins of a gazette. (The British make it hard even for mail to enter the city.) It cheers me to hear from them, and best of all, Daddy writes that come spring I may come home, for surely by then the city shall be free again. Thankful says she will miss me (will she really?), but I shan't miss a thing ~ least of all Aunt's endless chores.

I needed no silver repairs, but on the way back from market, I stepped into Mr. Revere's shop. I am not sure what I wanted except to feel part of the fight for Liberty.

This shows the Boston Massacre, when regulars fired into a crowd, killing five people. I love to hear Aunt tell the story ~ she is very dramatic and the wattles on her neck flap with indignation.

March 5, 1775

Today marked the 5th anniversary of the Boston Massacre. We went to hear Dr. Warren give the oration at Old South Church. When we got there, we found to our surprise that British officers (Thankful's

Old South Church

George among them) sat in the best seats. The hall was so packed
we stood at the back, and Dr. Warren himself could enter only by
climbing through the window behind the pulpit.

The good doctor was dressed in a white toga, gesturing with a
white handkerchief. Aunt Harmony heartily applauded his
appearance. She said it made a statement about the nobility of
our ideals, harking back to the ancient Romans (who evidently
wore togas). Amos said that was fine as long as he did not have
to dress that way.

The redcoats heckled and hissed as the Doctor spoke, but he ignored
them, recalling the brutality of the British firing into a crowd of
innocents. One captain, sitting on the steps beside Dr. Warren, held
up a handful of bullets defiantly, but the Doctor merely dropped his
handkerchief over the balls and went on with his speech, composed as ever.

He had scarcely finished (to loud applause) when one of the regulars
shouted, "Fire! Fire!" I thought there surely was no fire ~ this
was just a device to sow panic, and panic people did. Hordes swarmed
out the windows, climbing down the gutters. To add to the bedlam,
just at this moment (did the British plan this precisely?), a regiment
marched past with drummers and fifers, and the people fell onto the

Dr. Warren's handkerchief

palm
of
shot

Mrs. Purdy, the stout alewife, fell on the big drum ~ luckily for her, not so luckily for the drummer.

soldiers. There was much cursing and cuffing, and I feared a re-enactment of the massacre, but no shots were fired. We made it home unharmed, though Aunt Harmony huffed and puffed for hours afterwards.

Aunt Harmony telling a British grenadier she would like to ring his nose

March 30, 1775

Something is brewing, what I cannot say. The very air is abuzz with more than humblebees. The regulars drill and march and march and drill as if readying for battle. Shall there really be one? I read months ago that a delegate to the Continental Congress, Patrick Henry, demanded, "Give me Liberty or give me Death!" What a choice we must make!

April 19, 1775

Last night I woke to drums beating, a sinister sound. None of us could sleep, wondering what it all meant. I prayed no harm would

come to my loved ones. Would even now my brothers be facing the redcoats? We passed a dreadful night of uncertainty. Daybreak brought no relief, but as the sun grew high, rumors abounded, more with each hour.

Thankful did not go to lessons today but stayed with me, miserable. A stable boy brought her a note this morning from George. It said he could not see her today as planned, as he must march out~for how long, he knew not. She pictures the worst, as do I. We try to cheer each other up with riddles and songs.

Later today (after sundown)

My neck was stiff from waiting nervously by the time Amos finally came to tell us the news. The British went out searching for arms stored in Concord. Paul Revere and Billy Dawes rode to warn the militia in time to hide the munitions. What 'tis shocking is not the search for weapons, but that the British opened fire ~ with LIVE SHOT! Yes, 'tis true, 'tis horribly true, the lobsterbacks fired upon <u>us</u>, our militia. They <u>killed</u> men at Lexington Green and again at Concord. Aunt Harmony fainted at the news. Thankful believes it not. Could our protectors truly turn against us?

lead shot

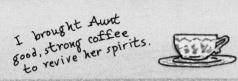
I brought Aunt good, strong coffee to revive her spirits.

Such news is horrendous enough ~ the hairs on my neck bristled as Amos spoke, but 'tis even worse, oh so much worse! As the British retreated to Boston, they plundered Menetomy. The regulars were brutes ~ bayonetting old men, forcing a woman in child-bed to flee naked with her new-born babe. My stomach turned to icy stone. How fared my family? I had to know! I clutched at Amos as though I could tear the answer from him but he knew not, and I fear the worst. I must go to my family. I must see them. I must find a way.

A LIST of the Names of the PROVINCIALS who were killed and Wounded in the late Engagement with His Majesty's Troops at Concord, &c.

KILLED.
Of *Lexington*
Mr. Robert Monroe,
Mr. Jonas Parker,
Mr. Samuel Hadley,
Mr. Jonas Harrington,
Mr. Caleb Harrington,
Mr. Isaac Muzzy,
Mr. John Brown,
Mr. John Raymond,
Mr. Nathaniel Wyman,
Mr. Jedediah Munroe.

Of *Menetomy*
Mr. Jason Russel,
Mr. Jabez Wyman,
Mr. Jason Winship,

April 26, 1775

I feel like a bird beating desperate wings against its cage.

Today is my chance to see my family! General Gage offered freedom of passage out of Boston today in exchange for weapons. People are streaming out of the city, I among them. Amos gave up an old blunderbuss (breaking it first so the British shan't use it against us) and took me with him. Every step nearer to Menetomy made my fears more vivid. I could not bear it if anything happened to Mamma, to Mercy, to any of them. Amos saw my worries and said that we, the colonists, are better prepared for such brutalities than

blunderbuss

Every day there is a new song mocking the British ~ now 'tis "Yankee Doodle," which was their song insulting us, the Yankees. Now 'tis their turn to be insulted by it. One new verse goes: "Dolly Bushel let a fart, Jenny Jones she found it, Ambrose carried it to mill, where Dr. Warren ground it." What that has to do with retreating lobsterbacks, I cannot say.

ever I suspected. (I did not know 'twas needed!) So much has been happening around me that I knew nothing of. For all the times that Dr. Warren visited us, I had no idea that he is the president of the Boston Committee of Safety. 'Twas he who directed the lantern signal and sent Mr. Revere and Mr. Dawes to alert the militia. (Both were captured by redcoats but let go.) That night Dr. Warren himself left Boston secretly by boat and joined in the fighting. A musket ball grazed his head, shooting off a lock of hair but mercifully leaving him unharmed. I drank coffee with a hero and did not know it! Amos says these times shall make heroes of us all, but when comes my time?

April 27, 1775

They are well ~ all well! Mamma and Daddy are the same as ever ~ how I flew from Amos's wagon into their arms. Then it was Mercy's turn, then Duncan's, John's, and Paul's. I had to hold each one a good long while, to feel their solid warmth, to smell their familiar scents. It was so odd, so wonderful, like sinking into a favorite feather bed, being back in our house, sitting at our table, hearing their voices again.

Over a good beef stew, we shared our news. Daddy spoke proudly of the militia, how well the cannon and shot had been hidden. Mercy was full of questions about Boston, but all I wanted to do was listen to her bright, piping voice.

The British found little for their pains and were surprised to see "country bumpkins" stand up to their polished might. Duncan, John, and Paul were full of tales of British cowardice, running back to Boston with their tails 'tween their legs liked whipped dogs. Mamma even had a story: After Colonel Prescott called out the minutemen, the women dressed in their absent husbands' clothes and, armed with muskets and pitchforks, set out to guard the bridge over the Nashua, determined to let no regular through. Sure enough, a soldier came by, carrying intelligence to the redcoats. The women searched him, found the reports hidden in his boots, and arrested him. When he realized his jailors were women, first he tried to bully them, then tried to flirt his way free. Both, laughed Mamma, failed. How I wish I had been there!

Then 'twas my turn to speak. Daddy was eager to hear news from Boston and what the British are planning. But I know nothing. I feel so useless. The times have made heroes of my family. When will my turn come?

Once again Mercy and I trade secrets in bed.

Another song making the rounds, poking fun at the redcoats:
"How brave you went out with your muskets all bright and thought to befrighten the folks with the sight,
But when you got there, how they powdered your pums, and all the way home how they peppered your bums,
And is it not, honies, a comical farce, to be proud in the face and be shot in the arse."

Mamma, Mercy, and I spent two days baking bread. Then we set it out on a long plank table by the side of the road, along with cheese and pails of cider. The militia men are crowding the roads, heading for Boston to face the British, and we wanted to feed them.

April 30, 1775

Tomorrow, Daddy says, I must go back to Boston. 'Tis safer there and Aunt needs me. I cannot bear parting with my family again, but I am only ten years old. I must do as I am told.

May 2, 1775

I am back in Boston but 'tis well, for now I hope to use the militia's secret code that Daddy has given me. If I discover any information on troop movements, I can be like Paul Revere and warn them! My ears are wide open. I await my chance.

The code is a diamond cut-out you lay over the letter to see the secret message. If the British found it, 'twould seem an innocent letter, though Daddy said I must also hide it well, as even the most innocent messages are confiscated.

Dear Mamma,
I hope that the farm is well and that you have men to reap the hay. Aunt H. is leaving me to cook supper for eight tonight. I have no help, for Concord, the hired girl, must go by the harbor to fetch some sea bass to serve. I must beware over-cooking, as Aunt is quite particular.
    Your loving daughter,
    Emma

May 3, 1775

Our neighbor Robert Newman has been clapped in jail. He is accused

Two lanterns meant the British were leaving Boston by sea; one meant they were going by land, through the Boston neck. Two lanterns were hung.

John, curled up in the wine butt

shirt

coat

breeches

waistcoat

of hanging the signal lanterns in Christ's Church. John Pulling is also suspected, but he escaped the soldiers searching for him by hiding in his grandmother's wine butt. (By the time he left his hiding place, he was quite drunk on the fumes.) Dr. Warren and Mr. Revere stay out of Boston or they, too, would be arrested. 'Tis a good thing the Continental Congress has created a new army, for now we must protect ourselves.

May 16, 1775

Thankful and I scarcely pass two words between us. She thinks me a traitor, and I think her a silly, lovesick goose. She pours out all her bitter abuse on me as I sit sewing clothes for our soldiers.

I pretend I do not hear her but think of Dr. Warren and Mr. Revere.

pocket

hose

May 20, 1775

Three cheers for Aunt Harmony! I long thought her old and frail, but today she was a fierce lioness. She heard from Sarah Owens that a merchant was selling coffee at inflated prices. Outraged, she gathered her quilting circle, and the group of women confronted the merchant, demanding coffee at reasonable prices. He, naturally, refused and told them to go back to their spinning

apron

mobcap

drawers

overskirt

wheels. So they set him a-spinning! They tied him up, carted him through town, to catcalls and hisses, all the way to his warehouse, where they lightened him of the weight of his keys, opened the doors, and relieved him of barrels of coffee. I think we have coffee now to last the winter!

May 25, 1775

Such hustle and bustle in the house today! Generals Clinton, Howe, and Burgoyne arrived, and we who had lived surrounded by redcoats must now live <u>with</u> them. General Burgoyne has claimed Aunt's house as his quarters. We are to stay in the upstairs chambers and leave him both the front and rear parlors. The kitchen is allowed ours, but only because he expects us to provide the meals for his table! We may provide him food, but he had best provide <u>me</u> with some information. I must use my code!

General Burgoyne is such a fop, 'tis hard to believe he is a general. He is more Macaroni than the Macaronis!

flat empty grain sacks

barrels of air

May 30, 1775

The advantage to housing a general is that we do not starve. Since Lexington, the city has been shut tight as a drum and though 'tis spring, and we should have cowcumbers, peas, squash, greens, and eggs, we have none. We live on salt fish, cheese, and Indian meal. But what I truly hunger for is news ~ anything to help the new army. I try to catch every word that escapes the General's lips, but so far 'tis all fatuous boasts and

Amos, bless his heart, brings us fresh fish when he can.

sneers about rough American ways ~ no intelligence from his pursed mouth. But still, I listen.

June 3, 1775

A letter from Mamma! Amos brought it to me with a firkin of fresh butter she sent us. She writes that our farm now houses sixteen people ~ the countryside is full of families come out of Boston, searching for a safe haven. Mamma could not refuse the women who came to her, babes in arms. I wish I could join them, be it ever so crowded! But I cannot abandon Aunt when she needs me most. She is determined to keep her property safe. Houses left by fleeing whigs are looted by the redcoats ~ or by Tories.

June 8, 1775

Thankful's pouty face with sour lips

At tea (real tea, courtesy of the General. Aunt and I pointedly drank coffee while Thankful threw us withering looks, like she had been fed on crab apples for a month), General Burgoyne boasted to Thankful that the American army is such a ragtag muddle of bumptious farmers, 'twould be a matter of weeks before they tired of playing at war and went home to their hayricks. I bit my cheek lest I speak out, but when I served the tea, somehow ~ by my faith I cannot imagine how! ~ my elbow was jarred, and some hot tea

Today Amos told me of a woman who hid a calf under her bed to keep the redcoats from taking it. She muzzled it with her petticoat to keep it from lowing and the soldiers did not discover it. Huzzahs for her!

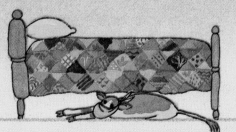

So this is how the General gets his beef!

poured onto the General's leg. Up he leaped, cursing my clumsiness (in not very gentlemanly language, I might add). I begged his pardon and rushed to wipe his breeches, but Thankful slapped me ~ slapped me! ~ and sent me from the room. Does she mistake me for her servant? Does she think herself Queen? I cannot bear her one more minute. I must think of some way to cook her bacon.

June 12, 1775

'Tis excessive hot today, making me even more ill tempered. I am still seething from Thankful's slap, but I have not yet fixed on how to avenge myself. Loosen the stitches on her petticoat so it falls to her ankles the next time she curtseys? Add vinegar to her tea? Place brambles neath her pillow? I have it! I shall add crushed, dried garlic to her hair powder~ how she shall reek after she does her hair!

June 13, 1775

'Tis done! Powder à la garlic. Woe to Thankful!

What a charming tea! Thankful kept turning her head, searching for the source of the stink. The General wrinkled up his nose and complained that something was "off." Thankful's face turned bright pink and she ran crying to her chamber.

June 16, 1775

I tremble as I write this, for if what I set down is seen by British eyes ~ or Thankful's ~ I am sure to be sent to prison. But this is

tankards of cool ale

the chance I have so long awaited. I must not hesitate.

Today General Burgoyne received the Generals Howe and Clinton, and, after sending me for cool cider (it being again unbearably hot), he bade me secure the door and allow no one to enter and disturb them. I meekly curtseyed and hurried upstairs. Fortunately, 'tis my chamber and not Thankful's that is over the front parlor, and I know that floor well. Expecting something momentous to be said ~ after near a month's wait ~ I glued my ear to a familiar knothole on the floor and could clearly hear their conversation. For once, 'twas not idle chatter!

my listening position

knothole

General Burgoyne laid out a plan for General Howe to land 1,500 men on the Dorchester peninsula and seize the heights south of the city. From there he would go on to attack the Americans at Roxbury. General Clinton, meantime, would attack from warships across the Back Bay and land on the banks of Willis Creek opposite the American army in Cambridge (where Dr. Warren is!). On such open ground, the troops would be sure of victory and would quash the rebellion in one day! The Sons of Liberty must know! Our army had to be saved. I thought of Amos. Yes, Amos! He was allowed on the water to fish ~ he could carry my news to Colonel Prescott,

needle

needle case

button form with letter folded inside and cloth sewn over it

Cambridge must get shipped

the leader of the militia camped in Cambridge. But how to get the word to him? The sentries always search boots and pockets. I looked around my chamber in despair — and then my eyes fell upon some button forms. Quickly I scribbled down what I had heard, using Daddy's code. ('Twas not as easy as I had thought to make it work!) Then I stuffed the paper in a hollow button form. My nervous fingers stitched up the button and slid it into my pocket with a threaded needle. I had only to find Amos, and all, I prayed, would be well.

I bumped into Thankful as I rushed downstairs, begged pardon as naturally as I could, forcing myself to slow my pace until I reached the kitchen. I told Aunt I was going to fetch more water, but as I stepped out, there stood Amos, as if he had heard my prayer.

"Why, Amos!" I cried. "Your button is loose. Let me remedy that for you." He looked perplexed, but as I quickly stitched, I whispered to him that he must get this button to Colonel Prescott at once. He thanked me and was off. And now? What will come of this?

June 17, 1775

Awoke to cannon fire, a desolate, terrifying sound. Aunt Harmony was sure the militia was attacking the city. The streets were full of turmoil — people

People clambered to the roofs and watched Charlestown burning as the redcoats stormed up the hill.

rushed hither and thither like chickens fleeing a fox. Then someone shouted that the fleet was bombarding Breed's Hill ~ the Americans had worked through the night to fortify the empty entrenchments there and were holding the heights. Now the British had to dislodge them. My heart flipped over when I heard that ~ it meant Amos had gotten through to the militia. My message was understood!

All of Boston was on the rooftops, watching the ships lob cannonballs at the rebels. The balls fell short and did little damage, but still they kept firing till almost noon. I prayed then that 'twas over, but 'twas only a brief respite. By two o'clock the cannonade had begun anew, now an incessant booming. The day was murderously hot, but I could not leave the baking roof.

At three o'clock the worst began. Not cannonballs now, but men, an ocean of men, streamed up the hill to the din of fife and drum whilst Charlestown was set afire with hot cannon shot. The Americans mowed down the redcoats in waves, and still the troops kept coming, stepping over their own dead, slipping in their comrades' blood. 'Twas horrible to watch. Aunt waited in the cooler darkness of the house, but Thankful stayed by me. She held my hand ('till it was soaked with sweat) and asked if my brothers were on Breed's Hill. I did not know but her

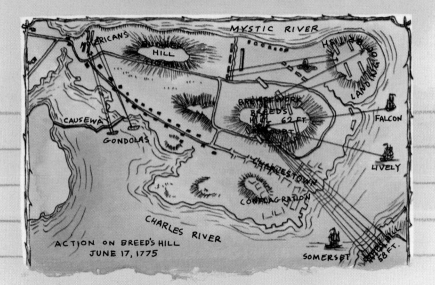

ACTION ON BREED'S HILL
JUNE 17, 1775

company eased me a bit, though I know she fretted over George, not my family.

Then something happened ~ I could not see what ~ but the militia stopped shooting and the British overran the fort. I could scarce believe 'twas over. Men lay dying on the slopes. Americans ran into the swamps and woods, fleeing the redcoats. Ashes from homes burning in Charlestown blew into my hair, my nose, my mouth. I was choking on the bitter dust of battle. I could not leave the roof but heaved up stomach bile and shook with great shuddering sobs.

Thankful held me, and we clutched each other, crying, each certain those we love lay bloody and beaten on the battlefield. Finally when our joints were stiff and all the tears had poured out of us, we stumbled back inside the house.

'Tis after supper. (I thought, "How could we eat?" But at least we made a show of sitting at table.) Amos has just left. He brought ugly news. Our soldiers stopped firing because they ran out of musket balls. But before they

mold to cast musket balls

Aunt goes to Sarah Owens's house for "cartridge bees" instead of quilting bees. The women use pine pitch for ammunition and melt down pewter for shot. Amos smuggles it out on his fishing boat, using my idea of hollow button forms to carry the ammunition.

fled. 1,000 redcoats lay wounded, more than 200 dead. Of the militia, 100 or so were killed, 300 wounded, and 30 taken prisoner. Although we lost the hill, Amos claims we won the battle. At too high a price, I fear.

June 18, 1775

I do not know about Daddy, John, Paul, or Duncan, but 'tis certain that Dr. Warren was killed. 'Tis hard to truly believe he is no more. I see him still, drinking coffee with us, eyes a-twinkle, so full of stories and excitement. I hear him finely orating in his toga at the commemoration for the Boston Massacre. He was a hero, bravely fighting at Concord and again at Breed's Hill. He was the last to retreat, defending the fort so others could escape. Rumor has it that Major Small (he of the peeled-onion eyes) called to the Doctor to give up, fighting against such odds was futile. Dr. Warren replied, "I am a dead man, fight on my brave fellows, for the salvation of your country." He died as he had lived~nobly, honorably. The British cruelly took off his fine silk waistcoat as a trophy ~ even General Burgoyne rowed over to see the body and crow over it. I cannot but wonder if 'tis my fault he died.

There is no body to bury for Dr. Warren. The British threw all the dead into a mass grave and will not allow a Christian service. Dr. Warren leaves a wife, 4 small children, and all of Boston to mourn for him.

Dr. Warren as I shall always see him

our last cone
of sugar

Oh, how I miss Dr. Warren! Aunt Harmony asked me to take her last sugar to his widow, but I could not face those fatherless children. I begged Amos to take it in my stead. I think he understands my sorrow.

June 23, 1775

What would I do without dear Amos? Today he brought me a letter from home, the good cheer I desperately needed! Thank the Lord ~ all are well! Daddy was grazed by a bullet but lost only some skin, and my brothers are fine. Mamma and Mercy have joined a company of women that goes from farm to farm, reaping the grain. Since all the men have left to join the army, the only way to harvest is for the women and children left at home to join together to do the work. I wish I, too, could work hard and simply and know I was doing the right thing. Spying is not so simple.

Amos also brought word that a general has been chosen to lead our army, a gentleman from Virginia named George Washington. I wonder at the choice of a southerner ~ they are said to be dissipated gamblers, evil slave owners. But Amos insists General Washington is dignity itself, a noble, upright leader. I trust 'tis so. We need no less.

July 12, 1775

I walked with Thankful to the city gates today, even though I am angrier than ever at her. Not for the slap or the way she has treated me but because she laughs with General Burgoyne, praising him for ridding the colony of rabble. "Such as that awful man, Joseph Warren," she said today. Aunt Harmony gasped in horror and I thought she would say something, but

Now 'tis easy to leave, but only if one takes very little ~ no furniture nor food may go. As the sentries inspected her cart, one woman tried to quiet her crying children with pieces of gingerbread. The cruel sentry snatched the morsels from the children and stuffed them in his own mouth! It sickened me to watch.

she simply excused herself from the room, claiming a sick headache. I would have kicked Thankful under the table, but she was too far away, so I excused myself as well and went to comfort Aunt.

August 8, 1775

Aunt Harmony and I went to meeting at Old South Church, but to our astonishment, General Burgoyne has made the church into a riding ring! The pews have been cleared out (all but one, which is now a pig sty), gravel has been carted in, and the Queen's Light Dragoons ride their horses there. I regretted not scalding the General more with that hot tea ~ I should love to pour it on his pompous pate!

Aunt was mad enow to eat the General whole without vinegar or sauce.

September 10, 1775

Thankful has been sad of late. Her uncle wants her to come home. She has written to him of George and insists she shall not leave him. She is a willful young lady, used to being indulged. She poured out her woes to the General, and he has gallantly offered to write to her uncle himself. How can her uncle refuse General Burgoyne? Everything that she wants falls into her lap. Even this war causes her no real suffering (aside from the dreary diet we all face). I cannot help myself ~ I hate her so! Then I wonder if I am just blaming all our misery on her, for while we are fettered, she seems free.

PROSPECT HILL	BUNKER'S HILL
I. Seven Dollars a Month.	I. Three Pence a Day
II. Fresh Provisions and in Plenty	II. Rotten Salt Pork
III. Health	III. The Scurvey
IV. Freedom, Ease, Affluence and a good Farm	IV. Slavery, Beggary, and Want

November 12, 1775

It has been long since I set pen to paper, but nothing happens worth recording. Besides, it has been too cold to write. All I would pen would be: "very cold today," "extremely cold," "exceeding cold," in short, "extremely excessive cold." So cold, that standing by the fire to warm my backside, the wet dishcloth in my hands froze.

November 23, 1775

On and on I spin and weave. We are starving, and still I am making cloth. I wish I could be truly useful, making cartridges at least. Shall I ever have the chance to use the code again, to help our rebellion?

I feel less "loyal" than ever. Yesterday General Howe, who is our governor since Governor Gage returned to England in September, sent out 300 men, women, and children, the poorest of the poor, homeless since the Almshouse was burnt down in Charlestown. He did not want them feeding off the King's stores, so he shipped them off to Chelsea, to find death either by cold or by starvation. General Burgoyne explained all this as if 'twere the most natural thing in the world. And Thankful agreed 'twas "eminently sensible." She calls such cruelty sensible? Her fashionable finery hides a cold, cold heart.

The Liberty Tree, the great elm which was our famous symbol of Freedom, was chopped down ~ whether for firewood or out of spite, I cannot be sure. The first effigies protesting Taxation without Representation were hung from this tree.

December 3, 1775

Which is worse, the cold or lack of food? Tonight we supped on potatoes and checkerberry tea. There are not three cows left in all of Boston. Nor much wood for fuel, either. All the fruit trees have been chopped down. (It shall be a bare, cheerless spring.) The West Church steeple has been taken down and used for kindling, as has all of the Old North Church. Governor Winthrop's ancient black house, which faithfully stood over 100 years, has been reduced to firewood. Whigs who left wooden houses empty will come home to bare earth. I should not wonder if we start burning <u>snow</u> in desperation.

January 8, 1776

'Twas a bit late to celebrate the dawning of a new year, but tonight I escaped the prison of the house, and I felt truly festive. The first performance of General Burgoyne's farce, <u>The Blockade of Boston</u>, opened at the new Faneuil Theatre. (He fancies himself a playwright as well as a general.) George invited Thankful, and I begged to go, too. I did not want to see ourselves mocked, but how I yearned to leave behind the bare cupboards and the cold hearth!

Thankful was elegant in a fine striped Persian gown, with a gauze cap and handkerchief (no need for <u>her</u> to boycott imported goods!), but I wore my best homespun and felt prouder than if I had worn Italian silk. I would describe the play, but we saw very little of it. Shortly after it began, an actor dressed as a Yankee sergeant ran on stage. He called for silence and said the alarm guns were fired ~ the rebels were attacking Charlestown, hammer and tongs. The audience applauded, but the Yankee insisted he was not play~acting, 'twas really so. We had only to go outside and see. That was a scene, as it dawned on the audience and the other actors that 'twas no fiction.

People trampled over the fiddlers, the actors called for water to wash the greasepaint off their faces as they charged off to duty, women shrieked and fainted, soldiers kicked and cursed. Thankful and I stayed seated to avoid the panicking throng. When the actor playing General Washington stumbled by, I called out, "Get those lobsterbacks, General!" He looked at me, confused, but Thankful pinched my arm and told him we were loyal subjects. I have put up with much from that girl, but no longer! I stood up on my chair and yelled," Three cheers for the American army!" Too bad by then the theatre was mostly empty. Thankful scowled at me and left huffily. Alone. I did not walk with her.

When I got home, Amos was in the kitchen, his eyes

pots of paint

This is how Thankful and I sit now when we sew in the same room. We cannot even look at each other.

'Tis not my fault, though Aunt urges me to be civil. Thankful despises me, my family, and what we fight for. What have I to say to her?

dancing with news. He said Washington had planned the bombardment just to disrupt the play. The farce had turned out to mock the British, not the rebels!

February 2, 1776

To add to our misery, the smallpox has broken out. Aunt Harmony determined that we should all be inoculated as 'tis much safer than contracting the pox naturally. I shall be cold, hungry, sick, and shut up with Thankful. I did not think things could get worse. But they have.

February 4, 1776

Dr. Rowe came this afternoon and stuck us with the pox. He said so many are taken sick, the whole city is quarantined, so we do not have to stay in the house. That is a small blessing. A bigger one is that the General has removed to Samuel Quincy's house. I no longer have to wait on him or suffer his insulting remarks, but with him goes my chance of overhearing any information.

February 27, 1776

'Tis the first day I feel well enow to write. Thankful has been herself nigh a week ~ lucky as ever, she ailed the least with nary a pox to mar her fine face. Aunt still lies abed and I worry that she is too old to withstand even this milder pox. 'Tis true she works me

There are fumigation pots at the city gates, and all who leave must first undergo a "smoking" to purify them of smallpox.

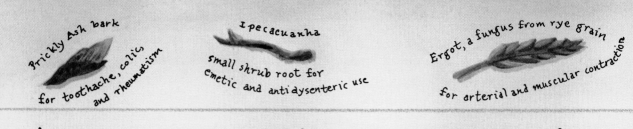

Prickly Ash bark
for toothache, colic
and rheumatism

Ipecacuanha
small shrub root for
emetic and antidysenteric use

Ergot, a fungus from rye grain
for arterial and muscular contraction

hard, but no harder than she works herself and I have grown truly fond of her.

February 28, 1776

I walked outside today for the first time in near a month. How still the city seems! But there are hints of spring. The ice is breaking in the river and I heard frogs peeping in the bog on the common.

When I first came to Boston ('twas a year and a half ago!), I was in awe of all the fine shops displaying their elegant wares and all the fashionable people walking the streets. Now those shops are bare or boarded up or torn down entirely. Well-dressed and -coiffed citizens no longer promenade (and now I know that finery does not make one a fine person). Instead there are carts loaded with coffins rumbling on the cobblestones, carrying off those who died of smallpox.

March 1, 1776

I think of our dear farm in Menotomy and how the kitchen garden must be sprouting, the fields greening, the sheep lambing, the cows big with calves. I pray my family is all well. 'Tis eight long months since I had any word from them.

March 2, 1776

At least without the General, Amos now visits freely. Today, bless

our farm

his soul, he brought me a letter from Mamma! She writes that they, too, were inoculated and are now recovered. Mercy has grown two inches and is a real help to her. Daddy and my brothers are serving under the command of Henry Knox, who I recall as a fat, prosperous bookseller here in Boston. Now he is leading a small army to Fort Ticonderoga to bring back the cannon captured from the British there. 'Tis a long journey (how will they manage to lug heavy artillery over snow, rough roads, woods, and rivers?), but Mamma has faith that all shall be well. I wish I could be as sure.

March 3, 1776

Last night I heard cannon fire. It lasted through the day. Is General Washington attacking Boston? What will happen to the innocent townspeople? First we suffered from the occupying redcoats, shall we now suffer from our own army?

Aunt Harmony is well again, once more reminding me, "Waste not, want not." She is her old self!

Thankful has changed the most. She is truly a young woman now.

She has confided to me that she hopes to wed George. She has written to her uncle for his consent.

March 5, 1776

I woke once more to fife and drum and ran outside to hear the news. The streets hummed with rumors ~ something was afoot. When the fog cleared, the sun shone on a new bulwark on the Dorchester Heights, bristling with cannon. The Americans had built it all under the cover of darkness, using the cannon I heard to distract attention from their efforts. 'Twas an astonishing work to be so quickly accomplished.

What did it all mean? I had to know. When Thankful slipped out for a tryst with George, I followed. Surely this time some intelligence would come from George, not just the usual billing and cooing.

I hid behind a rain barrel and strained to listen. After the hand kissing and the declarations of troth, my ears pricked up. George reassured Thankful that the rebels would not storm the city.

"We have strewn crow's feet on the road to Boston," he boasted. "They shan't be able to rush in, but must wend their way carefully and slowly. Time enough for us to leave, if need be."

Crow's feet? I knew not what they were, but I had to warn the army. I ran home and quickly wrote a few lines in Daddy's code, then stuffed the note in a button form. Off I raced to find Amos. I went from tavern to tavern until at last, at the Pig and Whistle, I saw his familiar form. I told him what I had heard as I sewed the button to his coat. "What are

E.FIBS' 1732

When General Howe saw the fortifications on the Heights, he exclaimed, "Good God, these fellows have done more work in one night than I could have made my army do in one month!"

Dearest Mamma,
How fare you and the farm? Have crows eaten all of the crops, slowing the harvest? Had I a way to help, I would!
From Boston,
your loving daughter,
Emma

crow's feet?" I asked, "and what does this new bulwark mean?"

Amos explained that the British will have either to retreat or surrender, for Washington has secured an impenetrable defense from whence his cannon can easily reach Boston. Cannon?! So Henry Knox succeeded, and Daddy and my brothers are near!

Amos said crow's feet are sharp, twisted metal prongs meant to lame a horse and slow an army down.

My news cheered Amos heartily. "If there are crow's feet, the British are planning a retreat, 'tis certain. And once our army knows to expect the the barbs, they shall quickly be prepared to clear them." Amos bowed low. "Another service you have done us."

Me? I blushed to think so. But as Amos bent over, I spied a necklace usually tucked neath his shirt but brought out by his bow. "What is that?" I asked, for 'twas a medallion of some sort, stamped with the Liberty Tree.

I saw a glint of gold around his neck.

Amos held up the medal to me. " 'Tis a secret sign that I am a member of the Sons of Liberty." He turned the coin over and on the other side were the words "Sons of Liberty" and an arm grasping a pole

This picture of Henry Knox and his men ~ my men ~ was in the Gazette. Mamma was right to have faith.

topped with a Liberty cap. My Amos? A Son of Liberty? I was so proud. I flung my arms around him and whispered in his ear, "Then hie thee, Son of Liberty, and get this button where it belongs. We have a war to fight!"

March 6, 1776

Amos ('tis hard to feel he is the same, now I know him to be a Son of Liberty) joined Thankful and me on the roof yesterday, watching to see what would happen. The British warships started bombarding the Heights, but as Amos predicted, the balls fell short and the ships soon gave up. Just before noon, we could see redcoats clambering aboard small transport boats and heading towards Dorchester, but no attack came. We supped on the roof, watching, waiting, but nothing happened. Finally at dusk, we came inside. It grew sharply cold and the winds rose. Had the British planned an attack last night, they must have been sorely disappointed, as a storm blew up. Will the ships try again today? Will the British retreat, and if they do, will they burn the city first? Rumors are thick, facts are scarce.

Thankful is beside herself. She sent for George, asking what she should do. I put my ear to the knothole in my chamber floor, eager to hear the British plans. Instead, I heard George ask Thankful to be his wife. And she said yes!

That girl is resourceful ~ she even had the approving letter from her uncle ready to show him. George laughed when he saw it, and said she has the Yankee spirit.

Thankful has packed her bags. She is so gay and lively, one would think she were setting off on a great adventure. (And so 'tis, I suppose) All the Tories are busily preparing to leave. Does that mean Boston shall be torched?

March 8, 1776

The tension is thicker than the spring fog. Washington is now setting mortars on Noddles Island, close to the northern shore. The Americans are surrounding Boston.

March 10, 1776

The harbor bristles with warships and the streets are sticky with molasses. The British are leaving, but not without a wake of spiteful destruction. I dare not leave the house or all in it will be plundered. Everywhere soldiers carry off linens and woolens, robbing what little is left us. Stores of salt and molasses are poured onto the cobblestones so we cannot use them. They take all they can carry ~ from tea sets to feather beds ~ and what they cannot hold, they break, burn, or throw into the harbor.

Coaches and furniture bob in the water like flotsam from some great shipwreck.

And they take the Tories who fear punishment, retribution, and ostracism. Thankful is gone, happy to be with George. She gave me a warm farewell and I tried to do the same. But I fear what will happen to us, we who stay.

Amos walked with me through the streets I now know well, but the city is so changed, it seems another Boston. Poor Old South Church reeks of manure. Broken chests and barrels are strewn everywhere. At least Aunt's house is whole.

A favorite Song Made on the Evacuation of the Town of Boston

Then hilterskilter they ran in the street, sometimes on their heads and sometimes on their feet,
Leaving cannon & mortars, packsaddles & wheat, Being glad to escape with the skin of their teeth.
Let 'em go, let 'em go, for what they will fetch, I think their great Howe is a miserable wretch;
And as for his men, they are fools for their pains,
So let them return to Old-England again.

March 17, 1776

The warships remain in the harbor, but the city is empty of soldiers. 'Tis quiet and still. I like it not.

March 18, 1776

The city gates are open and already the army is marching in. Amos said my warning gave the General an early start. He brought in horses and oxen to clear the crow's feet, so their advance was not much slowed. I have done something useful after all!

I search the ranks for a familiar face. So far I have seen some of the most noted Boston Whigs, such as Paul Revere and Reverand Cooper, but not Daddy, not yet.

March 20, 1776

They are here ~ Daddy, Duncan, Paul, and John! They sit in Aunt's parlor and I cannot believe they are truly here. They are so much bigger and louder than I recall. They fill the room with their chatter and laughter, their big boots and broad shoulders.

They entered the city following General Washington and Henry Knox (now an artillery colonel). I was gaping at the General, as regal as a king,

Daddy | John | Paul | Duncan

when Duncan stepped before me and scooped me up in a great bear hug. What a joyous reunion!

March 24, 1776

Amos came to dinner. Now that the gates are open, food is plentiful, but prices are high and Continental dollars are not welcome. Still we celebrated with a feast ~ a huge rump of beef, just enough corned to be said to be corned and no more, potato pudding, cheese, pease, muskmelons and cider. Amos offered a toast to me for discovering the crow's feet. Daddy arched an eyebrow at me and chuckled. "So you used the code? Well done! You made our last miles much easier, and after you have already walked 600 miles, each inch matters."

Children rushed to touch his coat, and women threw roses at his feet.

I could not stop grinning.

March 27, 1776

The British fleet is gone! Ten days they sat there, worrying us. Amos says they were just waiting for favorable winds. Daddy says they wanted to see what our army would do. Whatever the whyfor, 'twas with great relief I watched them disappear.

Continental currency~ more used to paper walls than wallets

TWENTYFOUR SHILLINGS

Issued in defence of American Liberty

Ense petit placidam sub Libertate Quietem

Aug.ᵗ 10 1775.

As a joke, someone dressed a dog in a collar of Continental bills. They have so little value, the dog could not even buy a bone with them!

April 4, 1776

General Washington left Boston and my brothers went with him.

The American general John Sullivan used a spyglass to watch the British garrison at Bunker Hill the day the redcoats took to their ships. There were still sentries posted at the fort, and he waited for them to leave. He waited and waited 'till finally he realized the sentries were not moving a hair. He led a party to the fort, and, sure enough, the sentries were dummies stuffed into British uniforms ~ a last British joke.

Daddy wants to take me home and see Mamma and Mercy. Then he will go, too. The battles may be over for Boston, but they are just beginning for the Colonies. 'Tis hard to bear the thought of another long separation but at least I shall have Mamma, Mercy, and the farm. I wish Amos would come with me. I must ask him.

April 8, 1776

A fine funeral was held for Dr. Warren today, near a year after he died. (Paul Revere identified the body, recognizing the false teeth he had made for the Doctor.) We followed the procession to the burial ground, and Dr. Warren was at last laid to rest.

I told Daddy about the warning I sent to Colonel Prescott before the battle of Breed's Hill, for I have long lain awake nights wondering if I did right. 'Twas because of me that so many good men died.

"But that was why I gave you the code, dove," Daddy said. "For just such news. 'Tis true that men died, but had the militia not been alerted, many more could have been lost, maybe even your brothers or myself. If you do nothing else during these hard times, you will have already done a great service for the Colonies and our cause."

I was crying, but Daddy wiped away my tears and held me like I was a little girl again. I do not know who I cried for, Dr. Warren or myself.

Dr. Warren, brought home

April 28, 1776

Amos came to bid me farewell. I begged him to come home with me, but he is following General Washington to New York.

"Now, Emma," he said, "would you deny me my chance to be a hero?"

"You are already a hero!" I protested. "You have done so much!"

"All I have done is carry messages and cartridges," he sighed. "Our country needs more. Like all you have done. You are a true Son of Liberty. You should be wearing this." And he took off his medallion and gently settled it round my neck. Then he kissed the top of my head. "When you see this medal, think of me and what we are fighting for."

I wanted to say thank you, but I could only nod my head and clutch the precious medal. Oh, Amos, I shall be worthy of it!

June 28, 1776

Soon 'twill be our turn to leave. Today Aunt found two new boarders and a hired girl. (May she live up to Aunt's standards of cleanliness better than I!) As soon as Daddy has finished helping round up the cannon left by the British and properly emplaced them, we shall be free to go!

July 18, 1776

At last, at last, tomorrow we leave for Menetomy! I am eager to

Amos was still a boy when first we met. Now he is a man. To me he is already a hero and always will be.

embrace Mamma and Mercy but 'tis well we were in Boston today for 'twas a great occasion I am happy not to have missed. This afternoon we went to the statehouse to hear the Proclamation of Independence. Two weeks ago the Continental Congress declared the Colonies a free country, severing completely our ties with England! I am no longer confused about how to be a British subject and still maintain our Liberties. The answer was stated so clearly and compellingly. I have never heard more inspiring words.

After the proclamation was read, the crowd cheered. There was a salute of 13 guns, taken up by cannon and muskets throughout the city. All the church bells clangored. Most stirring of all, though, was a group of boys, all around my age, playing fife and drum as they marched in step before the militia. They were so disciplined, with brisk movements, all in rhythm, and the music they played brought a flutter to my stomach, a quickening to my blood.

I thought of Amos, of the country he was helping to build. I was proud that I, too, had done something. When the boys started marching through the streets of Boston, Daddy, Aunt Harmony, and I fell in step behind them. We were all part of something greater ~ not just of Boston, or the Massachusetts colony, but of a new country, the United States of America.

IN CONGRESS. JULY 4, 1776.

The unanimous Declaration of the thirteen united States of America,

WHEN in the Course of human Events, it becomes necessary for one People to dissolve the Political Bands which have connected them with another, and to assume among the Powers of the Earth, the separate and equal Station to which the Laws of Nature and of Nature's God entitle them, a decent Respect to the Opinions of Mankind requires that they should declare the causes which impel them to the Separation.

We hold these Truths to be self-evident, that all Men are created equal, that they are endowed by their Creator with certain unalienable Rights, that among these are Life, Liberty, and the Pursuit of Happiness—That to secure these Rights, Governments are instituted among Men, deriving their just Powers from the Consent of the Governed, that whenever any Form of Government becomes destructive of these Ends, it is the Right of the People to alter or to abolish it, and to institute new Government, laying its Foundation on such Principles, and organizing its Powers in such Form, as to them shall seem most likely to effect their Safety and Happiness. Prudence, indeed, will dictate that Governments long established should not be changed for light and transient Causes; and accordingly all Experience hath shewn, that Mankind are more disposed to suffer, while Evils are sufferable, than to right themselves by abolishing the Forms to which they are accustomed. But when a long Train of Abuses and Usurpations, pursuing invariably the same Object, evinces a Design to reduce them under absolute Despotism, it is their Right, it is their Duty, to throw off such Government, and to provide new Guards for their future Security. Such has been the patient Sufferance of these Colonies; and such is now the Necessity which constrains them to alter their former Systems of Government. The History of the present King of Great-Britain is a History of repeated Injuries and Usurpations, all having in direct Object the Establishment of an absolute Tyranny over these States. To prove this, let Facts be submitted to a candid World.

He has refused his Assent to Laws, the most wholesome and necessary for the public Good.

He has forbidden his Governors to pass Laws of immediate and pressing Importance, unless suspended in their Operation till his Assent should be obtained; and when so suspended, he has utterly neglected to attend to them.

He has refused to pass other Laws for the Accommodation of large Districts of People, unless those People would relinquish the Right of Representation in the Legislature, a Right inestimable to them, and formidable to Tyrants only.

He has called together Legislative Bodies at Places unusual, uncomfortable, and distant from the Depository of their public Records, for the sole Purpose of fatiguing them into Compliance with his Measures.

He has dissolved Representative Houses repeatedly, for opposing with manly Firmness his Invasions on the Rights of the People.

He has refused for a long Time, after such Dissolutions, to cause others to be elected; whereby the Legislative Powers, incapable of Annihilation, have returned to the People at large for their exercise; the State remaining in the mean time exposed to all the Dangers of Invasion from without, and Convulsions within.

He has endeavoured to prevent the Population of these States; for that Purpose obstructing the Laws for Naturalization of Foreigners; refusing to pass others to encourage their Migrations hither, and raising the Conditions of new Appropriations of Lands.

denounces our Separation, and hold them, as we hold the rest of Mankind, Enemies in War, in Peace, Friends.

We, therefore, the Representatives of the UNITED STATES OF AMERICA, in GENERAL CONGRESS, Assembled, appealing to the Supreme Judge of the World for the Rectitude of our Intentions, do, in the Name, and by Authority of the good People of these Colonies, solemnly Publish and Declare, That these United Colonies are, and of Right ought to be, FREE AND INDEPENDENT STATES; that they are absolved from all Allegiance to the British Crown, and that all political Connection between them and the State of Great-Britain, is and ought to be totally dissolved; and that as FREE AND INDEPENDENT STATES, they have full Power to levy War, conclude Peace, contract Alliances, establish Commerce, and to do all other Acts and Things which INDEPENDENT STATES may of right do. And for the support of this Declaration, with a firm Reliance on the Protection of divine Providence, we mutually pledge to each other our Lives, our Fortunes, and our sacred Honor.

John Hancock

Button Gwinnett
Lyman Hall
Geo Walton

Wm Hooper
Joseph Hewes
John Penn

Edward Rutledge

Thos Heyward Junr.
Thomas Lynch Junr.
Arthur Middleton

George Wythe
Richard Henry Lee
Th Jefferson
Benja Harrison
Thos Nelson jr.
Francis Lightfoot Lee
Carter Braxton

Samuel Chase
Wm Paca
Thos Stone
Charles Carroll of Carrollton

Robt Morris
Benjamin Rush
Benja Franklin
John Morton
Geo Clymer
Jas Smith
Geo Taylor
James Wilson
Geo Ross
Caesar Rodney
Geo Read
Tho McKean

Wm Floyd
Phil Livingston
Frans Lewis
Lewis Morris

Richd Stockton
Jno Witherspoon
Fras Hopkinson
John Hart
Abra Clark

Josiah Bartlett
Wm Whipple
Saml Adams
John Adams
Robt Treat Paine
Elbridge Gerry
Step Hopkins
William Ellery
Roger Sherman
Saml Huntington
Wm Williams
Oliver Wolcott
Matthew Thornton

The people Emma describes in her journal are for the most part fictional—Amos, Aunt Harmony,
Thankful, and everyone in Emma's family. But some key people in the book really existed
and played important roles in the American Revolution. Paul Revere, Benjamin Franklin,
Patrick Henry, George Washington, and, on the British side, Governor Gage and Generals Clinton,
Howe, and Burgoyne are all well-known figures of the Revolution. Colonel Prescott, William Dawes,
John Sullivan, Robert Newman, John Pulling, Henry Knox, and Dr. Joseph Warren may be less-familiar
names, but each of them made important contributions, especially Dr. Warren, who died in the
battle of Breed's Hill (later known as the battle of Bunker Hill).

ISBN 0-439-20351-1

Copyright © 1999 by Marissa Moss. All rights reserved.
Published by Scholastic Inc., 555 Broadway, New York, NY 10012,
by arrangement with Harcourt Brace & Company. SCHOLASTIC and
associated logos are trademarks and/or registered trademarks
of Scholastic Inc.

12 11 10 9 8 7 6 5 4 3   1 2 3 4 5/0

Printed in the U.S.A.   23

First Scholastic printing, September 2000

The illustrations in this book were done in watercolor, gouache, and ink.
The text type was hand lettered by Marissa Moss.
The display type was set in Pabst.

Designed by Lydia D'moch and Emma

Author's Note

Although there is no record of a ten-year-old girl spying for the American rebels, many women did spy during the revolution. Emma's adventure of overhearing battle plans and sneaking information out in hollow buttons is modeled after Lydia Darragh's experience. Lydia listened through a crack in the floor when the British requisitioned a room in her house for a council chamber. While many women, like Lydia, spied when opportunity presented itself, others actively organized themselves against the British. The biggest spy ring ~ the Culper Ring of New York ~ was run by men, but many of its operatives were women. One spy, Anna Strong, used her clothesline to signal the rebel army when it was safe to land on Long Island; when a black petticoat flapped in the wind alongside a certain number of white handkerchiefs, the rebels knew that the coast was, literally, clear.

To get as close as I could to the revolutionary experience, I read many diaries of the period, particularly those of girls and women. The two that influenced me most were Anna Green Winslow's and Sally Wister's. Anna, who was staying in Boston with her aunt to be "finished," provided the model for Thankful. But while Anna appears shallow, caring only about clothes and frolics, Sally seems spirited and mischievous, aching for excitement. I wanted Emma to share Sally's humor, warmth, and irreverent spirit.

I was especially touched by how diarists expressed their confusion over national identity: Should they be loyal to the British crown or to the colony they lived in? These complex issues played out in every meeting house. The American Revolution first occurred in people's hearts and minds as they, like Emma, began to see themselves not as British subjects but as *Americans*, belonging to a new, fiercely independent nation.